The GREAT HAMSTER GETAWAY

Lou Carter

Magda Brol

BLOOMSBURY
CHILDREN'S BOOKS
LONDON OXFORD NEW YORK NEW DELHI SYDNEY

Raffleton Grey was as bored as could be,
with nowhere to go and nobody to see.

His round-and-round wheel never went anywhere.
His house in the corner was gloomy and bare.
The food was so tasteless he turned up his nose.
The wood shavings always got stuck in his toes.

And so he would dream every day to be free,
to run on the pebbles and splash in the sea.

To snooze by the harbour and breathe in the air

and gobble up crumbs
people dropped at the fair.

"It's time!" he declared as he gazed at the stars.
"Tomorrow's the day I'll escape from these bars!"

His plan was quite simple
and all he would need

was a roll in his ball
and a sunflower seed –

a nudge from the cat,

a bump from the chair,

a seesaw,

a duck . . .

. . . and he flew through the air.

Through branches and leaves

he

came

tumbling

down

and landed beside something scruffy and brown.

It scuttled and hid
in the shade of the tree,
and Raffleton gasped,
"You're a HAMSTER . . .
          like ME!

No need to be frightened –
I'm Raffleton Grey."
And then he said proudly,
"I'm running away!"

The other one smiled,
"I'm Puckerford Brown.
I've run away too
from my owner in town."

The two little hamsters were **finally free.**

They **ran** on the pebbles
and **splashed** in the sea.

They **snoozed** by the harbour
and breathed in the air,

then **gobbled up** doughnuts
they found at the fair.

They danced
and they **sang**

and they rode
all the rides . . .

They feasted
on ice cream

and slid

down the slides.

It really had been a spectacular day . . .
but then it grew dark as the sun slipped away.

The two little hamsters
began to feel worried
and eyes seemed to follow
wherever they hurried.

All through the night
they were **chased by the cats,**

followed by foxes

and seagulls . . .

. . . and rats.

By morning they just couldn't run anymore.
The two little hamsters flopped down on the floor.
And Raffleton said, "I don't like being free!
It's not as much fun as I thought it would be!"

What would become of them out in the wild!
They sat, and they wondered . . .

. . . then Raffleton smiled!

"I know," he said, "of a wonderful place.
It's not far away and it's perfectly safe!"

Their plan was quite simple and all they would need
was an old piece of rope . . .

and a twang
from the tree –

a bounce
on the cat,

a fling from the gnome,

a sponge,

a balloon . . .

... and at last they were home!

"We MADE it!"

cheered Raffleton, darting about.

"The food is DELICIOUS and never runs out!
We'll snooze in the house, have a wood-shaving fight
and run in the round-and-round wheel EVERY night."

Raffleton Grey didn't want to be free,
to run on the pebbles or splash in the sea.

"I don't need the crumbs people drop at the fair.
I don't need the harbour or seasidey air.

I think I was lonely and needed a friend."

So everything turned out all right in the end.